HE GOT ME

Tyson

JUST BAE

CONTENTS

It's a Wednesday afternoon when Tyson Jackson facetimes his on-again off-again girlfriend, Veronica Hayes. Her finger hovers over the decline button, "What does this boy want now?" Veronica looks at his fingernails. "I needed my nails done like yesterday."

"Hello."

"Veronica!"

"Facetime me on audio. My hair's a mess."

"Give me a second. I'm driving."

"Don't break the law."

"I won't." Tyson switches over to audio.

"Veronica."

"Hello, you called?"

"Stop with the funny shit. How's your summer break going?"

"It's going…"

"Well, I was thinking since you're here in Atlanta, why don't you stay at my parents' place until you get your dorm room. It's cheaper than Motel 6."

Veronica looks around the room at the piles of clothes in the corner.

"I'm good fine for now. Your parents don't know me like that."

"But I do. When's the last time you had a home-cooked meal? I know video games and Chinese food every day get kinda dragged out?"

"Well you know me, all too well except you don't—"

"What's that suppose to mean?"

"Tyson—"

"Veronica—"

"I gotta go."

"I'll be in town tomorrow. I'm coming by to pick you up."

"No, you're not."

"What did I say?"

"Bye, Tyson."

It didn't use to be like this but somewhere along the way right before Veronica graduated high school, she and Tyson lost something. They messed around a few times when Tyson was playing ball in Miami before Veronica moved to Atlanta. Then, he just popped two months ago at her graduation. Tyson was a star basketball player in college when he met Veronica at one of his games.

———

Tyson got all dressed up when he came to get Veronica. She hugged him for a quick second and said, "That's enough."

"I missed you."

"Me too. Now where we going?" Veronica kept checking out his Georgia Tech sweatshirt.

"To the Underground first. I know Miami ain't got good barbecue like the A."

"You paying right?"

"Wouldn't you want to know?"

"Stop playin' Tyson. I hate you boy!"

They walk hand in hand but stop at a coffee shop first.

"I'm still getting used to this new Atlanta. It's different."

"I remember coming downtown when I came to see my folks when I was younger. Since I moved here, I rarely come down here."

After getting two lattes, Tyson asks Veronica about her soccer scholarship at Georgia Tech."

"I'm glad they gave a sista some money. I really want to try out for the USA Women's soccer."

"You'll make it."

"I'll try."

"I know you will. Remember this." Tyson pulls up a picture of her in her high school soccer uniform holding up a championship trophy.

"Damn, you still got that?"

"You act like I forgot about you."

"Don't even start, Tyson."

"Whatever."

They get in the car and head to the Underground and Lamont, Veronica's friend from school texts her.

"What's up with your cousin, Shanae Nae? Nigga out here drunk."

Veronica laughs and texts back, "LOL."

"What's so funny?" Tyson said looking at the road.

"Nothing except Lamont texting me about my cousins."

"That nigga still ain't working yet."

"Leave him alone, Tyson. We just graduated high school."

They pull up and park near the Underground.

"Oh yeah, I wanted to know if you're going to busy tomorrow?"

Veronica puts her phone away. "Not really, why?"

"Take a ride out with me to Tybee?"

"What's Tybee?"

"A beach here. "You remember my boy Tony?"

"Yeah, the fat light-skin dude?"

"Yeah. He's got a beach house for a few days and he's going to be with his girl there. They need some company."

"Tony's got a girlfriend?"

"I said the same when I heard him tell me."

They order some food and suddenly, Veronica decides she rather eat at home. On the ride back, she daydreams about all the things Tyson can do to her at Tony's house. It feels like she's sixteen again. She thinks about laying on Tyson's bed, smokin' a blunt and then getting fucked. The scene would play out like:

"Daddy, daddy, you got me cumming so much. Stop! Stop! Oh my God! Right there, Right there, Oh Shit! Ah! Oh! Ohhhhhh!"

Tyson would say, "Shush, you're going to get me locked up."

They'd at her mom's house when she cut school.

Veronica's heart aches every time she thinks of Tyson fucking her young pussy. He's been her little boo thing on the low since he stopped going out with a junior who wanted to be an Instagram hoe at her school.

"So we're going to be with Tony and his girlfriend?"

"Yeah, a foursome, as they call it."

"So, you mean we're sleeping all in the same room?"

"If you want."

"Tyson, you know me better than that. I ain't no hoe."

"Just joking. We'll have our own room."

"Tyson—don't play with me."

"I'm not." Tyson pulls up to Motel 6 to drop Veronica off. "I'll come around noon tomorrow to scoop you up. Be ready." He kisses Veronica on the cheek and she gets out.

"Ok, Tee."

CHAPTER TWO

Tyson's shirt is halfway buttoned when he picks Veronica up. It's hot, close to ninety degrees already. He's rocking some Porsche Designs, looking fly.

"What's up with the star-studded appearance?"

"Just trying to look fresh, baby. That's all."

"Look at those sandals? You're killing it."

"Being the man means you have to dress like one."

"Don't let it go to your head."

"Yeah, yeah!"

Tyson grabs her handbag off the carousel when Veronica points to it.

"And being a man means wearing sandals?"

"Nah."

"I thought so."

Tyson's sunglasses are tangled in Veronica's hair when he reaches down to kiss her.

"You smell good baby."

"You do, too."

————

Tyson rented a red Ferrari convertible and Veronica's hyped.

"Got it to fuck with Tony!"

"I see." Veronica puts on her sunglasses and plops her feet up on the dashboard.

"So, listen," Tyson said as he pulls out of the parking lot, "Tony and his girl are in the midst of getting back together—"

"Okay—"

"I heard them earlier arguing and shit, or well, I heard her, anyway. I figured we'd give them some time before we show up. So, we got an extra night."

"Here you go," Veronica said, putting her hand over her face. "I knew you were up to something."

"I wasn't."

"So, you're just going to drive around."

"Hmm, I know where I'm taking you."

"Where?"

"My secret."

————

They drive to a nearly empty parking lot on the top floor of Publix a few miles away. Veronica drank a Corona on the way and is feeling tipsy.

"Is this where you wanna fuck?"

"You're on, already. It only took one beer."

"You mean it only takes one good beer—" Veronica slurs coming down the staircase wobbling. Tyson's holding her and she's giggling.

"How far are we from where you stay?"

"Haha, you mean how far are your dorms from here?"

"You're so funny—"

Tyson knows downtown well; it was his hangout for four years in university; the sports bars, clubs, and strip clubs. They walk through the parking lot to an old eighties school bus parked outside with graffiti written on it.

"Sam's Soul Food? Can't get more ghetto than this?"

"Haha, I see you got jokes."

———

Once they're seated, Veronica asks, "Is this your favorite place to eat?"

"Honestly, I've never been here. My boy, Willie said they got good ribs."

"Word to the brotha, Willie!" Veronica said laughing so hard, everyone looks at her.

"I see you got jokes."

"Of course, Tee."

———

They order a dozen ribs, fries, and few drinks and although the ribs are small, Veronica is stuffed. She drank a few more Coronas feeling like she needed to be rolled out of the restaurant.

"I could sleep right here. I'm so done."

"I see."

"What you say?"

"Nothing. Let's head out."

Tyson pays and walks out first. He's walking fast and Veronica jogs to catch up.

"Wait, wait. What did I do?" She grabs Tyson's arm. "Talk to me."

"Nothing."

"What's on your mind then?"

"Nothing."

"Spit it out or else."

Tyson sighs, pulling out some tickets. "I've got these to see the Braves tonight."

"Okay and—"

"You coming?"

"Tyson, I ain't trying to be around all those white people.

"Come on, babe. Get yo head out of the gutter. Let's do something different.

"What time does the game start?"

"In thirty minutes."

"Ok, you got me."

———

"We're in the wrong section," Tyson said looking at the tickets.

"No, we're not."

"If you don't stop with the foolishness."

"We're sitting here until they kick us out. Matter of fact, go get me a cold one, some nachos, and a Braves hat."

"Nigga, you really feeling yourself."

Veronica ignores Tyson and sings, "Take me out to the ballgame. Take me out to the game."

"Now you wanna be a fan?"

"Go ahead, boy. I'm hungry."

"Give me some money."

"You're rich."

———

They watch the Braves lose to the Detroit Tigers but spend most of the time joking and talking. Tyson bought Veronica a Braves finger, and she kept poking him with it.

Since they have a night to play around, Tyson convinces Veronica to spend the night out at parents' house who are out of town for the weekend.

On the way home, Veronica falls asleep in the car. The breeze blows and Tyson sings poorly to whatever's on the radio.

"We're here.".

"Pick me up. I can't walk."

"Only if you ask nicely."

He remembers the time they snuck out after Veronica's curfew. It was their first nightout and Tyson was so drunk that he fell on his face. Veronica stole a bottle of E & J from her mother's mini-bar and had her first drink. She also came so much that night that she could hardly walk in the morning.

Tyson holds Veronica at the waist, up the stairs to his sister's room who left home to work in New York a year ago. He opens the door and it's dark except for the light from the windows. He sets down her bag and flips on the lamp.

"This bed's so cozy. Are you going to keep me company tonight?"

Tyson ignores.

"The bathroom's over there and my room's down the hall."

"I—said," Veronica stutters.

"You said you're going to bed."

"All right—"

———

They headed up to Tony's and his girl, Gina for two days and Veronica and Tyson had a ball. Tony told Tyson that this young girl would get him in trouble after seeing Veronica coming out of the pool.

"OG, I'm the one driving and she's riding," Tyson said sipping on a Pina Colada.

"My nigga, that body is a muthafucka…"

"Hey y'all, we be back," Gina said pulling Veronica along.

"Yeah, we be back," Veronica repeated looking dumb.

"Don't get lost," Tyson said looking at Veronica's booty.

"You heard the man, Gina," Tony said sticking out his tongue.

The girls went driving around Tybee while the boys were out in the back of the condo barbecuing. Later that evening, they watched a movie together then the real fun started; sounds of the foursome fucking as if they were competing with one another.

"Tony, Tony! Fuck me, fuck me, hit this pussy. Oh my God, I'm cumming" was heard from one room.

"Daddy, daddy, don't stop! Right there, Oooh! Oooh! I'm about to—" from the other room.

In the morning, everyone laughed about it at breakfast.

———

When they got back from Tybee, Veronica was so relaxed. She went back to Motel 6 instead of Tyson's and went to bed early. She dreamt about the first time Tyson came to her house when she was in her senior year in high school and what happened after that. Her mother was working the night shift that week.

"Vee?" Tyson knocked on the door.

"What?" Veronica looked up from her phone. Her cousin, Lamar texted her from the other room, "Come on, Cuz. Let's go to the store before somebody have you for dinner."

"You're so wrong. He's just a friend," Veronica texted back.

"Why are you up here? I told you to stay downstairs, Tyson."

"I can't sit on that raggedy-ass couch. That shit's hurting my ass."

"And that's my problem, how?"

Veronica let him crash the night at her place even though he was fucking with Tanya at her school.

"I got Finals tomorrow. Give a kid a break."

"Why are you over here again?" Veronica sighed, "Ok," patting the bed for Tyson to come.

Tyson leaped from the door to her bed in seconds and curled up next to Veronica.

"What's all that for?"

"You always got something extra to say."

"Anyway, the heat's off. My mom didn't pay the bill again on time this month."

"Got another pillow?"

"There's two in the closet."

Tyson looked at Veronica signaling to get him one.

"Get your butt up and get me one."

Tyson does and comes back to bed.

"Close the door and turn off the light. This isn't going to become a habit, is it?"

Tyson hums.

"I mean it, Tyson. You can't just come in here whenever you like. You got a girlfriend named Tanya and this shit doesn't look right."

"I'll think about it."

"I said what I said and I mean it. As long as you fuckin' that hoe—"

"She ain't no hoe.

"Whatever."

"Well, it won't be long before it's over."

"Yeah, right."

Tyson fell asleep within minutes while Veronica watched. She rubbed his chest and wanted to play but didn't want him to miss his exams.

The alarm went off at 5:30 AM and Tyson's arm was wrapped around Veronica. He was blowing hot hair on her neck and it felt so good.

Veronica didn't pull his arm off her. Tyson's dick was poking Veronica in her butt.

Tyson woke up seconds later rolling over.

"Good morning, Tyson."

"Morning."

"I'm going to say this one time and one time

only: you better not ever wake up next to me with that thing down there poking me."

"Young girl, stop while you are ahead." Tyson got up.

"I mean it. I'm not playing with you."

"I'll talk to you later. Thanks for letting me crash at your place."

"Pass your exams and call me later. Good luck!"

Veronica fell back asleep into the warmth of the spot Tyson left behind.

———

Lisa, Shanae's girlfriend, is in the kitchen later that morning making smoothies in her sister's t-shirt and panties and offers Veronica one.

"Tyson didn't tell you he moved here to be closer to the girls he's been fucking with at your school."

Veronica shakes her head, taking a sip. "There's too much banana in this, girl."

"You're funny." Lisa hops onto the barstool next to Veronica. "I ain't lying. Word around here is that everybody wants a piece of Mr. Tyson."

Veronica laughs. "I only know one and that's the junior Ms. Instagram. We're only friends."

"Friends, huh?"

"Yes, I said, 'friends'. I ain't give him no pussy—yet."

"Did you just say 'yet'," Lisa pokes out her lips. "That nigga gonna get some, watch!

"Well, I don't have no control over that but if he does, it's because he worked for it. This pussy ain't free."

"I hear you, girl. Just don't get your little ass knocked up."

"Please..."

"I'm telling you, don't."

Lisa drinks as Veronica daydreams about to do if Tyson comes over again.

"So, when's Tyson coming over again?"

"Never, it was just once."

"Once, huh?"

"He got a girl."

Lisa hums. She doesn't believe a word Veronica's saying.

———

But Tyson came over again after his exams and Veronica's in the backyard pool. She was taking selfies of her booty and sending them to a boy named LaMont who she used to fuck with in school.

"Is this too much ass showing?"

"Damn, your ass' looking good," he texts back.

"I ain't fuckin' with you. I just asked you a question."

"You ain't right, mommy."

———

Veronica gets butterflies when she sees Tyson coming inside and sitting on the couch.

Veronica's brother, Man-Man does a double-take when Veronica comes in.

"Mr. is here for you?"

"Please, Man-Man, go. You got too much energy for me."

Lisa comes in seeing Veronica drying off.

"Okay, Ms. Legs," Lisa looks Veronica up and down and then over to Tyson.

"Hi, Tyson."

"Hi, Veronica."

Veronica goes back out to the pool and Tyson eyes that young booty hitting the water before he goes in.

———

It rains in the afternoon right after Tyson gets in the pool. They hurry inside and cuddle up while Veronica starts up her cousin Lamar's PS4.

"Want to put something on?" Tyson said seeing Veronica shivering. The air conditioning is on blast.

"Well, I don't feel like going upstairs. God knows what Lisa and Shanae are doing up there."

"Here," Tyson gives her a blanket from the couch.

They take turns playing Mortal Kombat for an hour.

"How's Monica?" Veronica said eating a mouthful of chips.

Monica was Tyson's junior girlfriend who was slim with a booty. The girl was a freak always in nigga's DMs.

"We're taking a break."

"A break?"

"She's just doing her thing."

"I'm sorry, it ain't working out."

"It's cool."

"So y'all still fuckin?"

"Nah."

"Stop lying."

"What about Lamont?"

"What? "I don't know what you're talking about."

"You know what I'm talking about."

"Do I?"

Tyson pushes the bag of chips away. "That nigga that you were fuckin at your school."

"What? We didn't fuck."

Tyson pulls his phone out, flipping through his messages while Veronica remembers exactly what she said to Tyson that night she was drinking. She had called him by mistake thinking it was Lamar.

"Guess who lost their virginity tonight, Lamar?" Tyson read.

Tyson was in his bed, playing along. "Tell me?"

"Ain't you nosy?" Veronica texted.

She had a couple of drinks and danced with Lamont and then when he asked Veronica to go upstairs, she followed.

"Seriously?" Tyson said holding in his laughter. "Then what happened."

"Nothing I would brag about."

"That bad, huh?"

"That nigga was sweatin' like a gorilla. It hurt so badly."

"Haha, I guess Lamont wasn't the pastor's son," Tyson texted laughing so hard.

Veronica then realized she had texted the wrong number and blocked the number.

———

Veronica never told Tyson that in her sophomore year, she explored some new things.

She crawled into bed with her one of her soccer teammates at school during one of their away competitions. The girl kissed Veronica and she kissed back. Then, things got steamier. The girl went down on Veronica, licking her pussy and fingerfucking her. She made Veronica say her name and Veronica felt like the victim.

They played again and again and again almost for a year every time they went away for matches. No one knew except for the two.

Yet, there were a lot of things Veronica hadn't told Tyson.

————

Veronica calls LaMont that night when Tyson leaves.

"Tyson knows," she said as soon as he answers.

"Well—"

"I said Tyson knows that me and you were fuckin around."

"Well—"

"What do you mean? Say something."

"I saw that nigga like two months ago."

"And—" Veronica sights.

"He came up to me saying he heard this and that—"

"And you didn't fuckin' tell me, yo?"

"I saw him at my cousin's crib, so I spit facts to him on the low. We good."

"And you just get to decide what to say?"

"He's my cousin's homie, Vee. Nigga like fam."

"So you rattin' now?"

"Oh, come on. As if you and Tyson haven't kissed and tell. Did you tell him about the little dyke thing you had goin' on?"

"Muthafucka."

LaMont shuts up and Veronica thinks for a moment he hung up on her.

"Hello—"

"Yeah."

"Why you tripping?"

"I'm not— "

"That nigga Tyson got your ass whipped. Shit, don't he fuck with that hoe at ya school?"

"Old school—he don't fuck with her no more. Did you even graduate?"

"I graduated from yo ass."

"So you liked eating it? That's what you saying."

"I did actually. Shit was the bomb."

"You're a nasty muthafucker." Veronica is actually turned on how Lamont sounds.

"So what are you going to do Tybo?"

"About who? Did you just call him Tybo?"

"About Tyson."

"Nothing..."

LaMont sucks his teeth. "Well, give the nigga some head. He might be a good dude."

"You're so fucking disrespectful."

"Seriously, I think y'all made for each other.

"That nigga is five years older than me."

"You're seventeen. In a year, it won't matter, Vee."

"Well, that's the best thing you've said all night."

"Alright, since you're proud of me, I'm coming over."

"No, thank you. I'll pass."

"Then, call me when it's over." Lamont bangs on her.

"This pussy's still mad he can't get none."

———

Veronica woke up seeing she was still on her mother's king-size bed. She went back to sleep dreaming about his fingers going in and out of her creamy pussy.

"Oh, Tyson! Oh, Tyson! Ooooh, I'm cumming..." Veronica shakes making herself cum and feels guilty afterward. Her mother's bed now has a wet stain and she'll be home from work in a few hours.

"Tyson's gonna get it. Watch," Veronica said when she woke up later that morning. She scrubbed the stain and then went downstairs to make herself a bowl of cereal. "Let me hit up, Letisha to see what she's up to."

CHAPTER THREE

*L*ater in the morning after they got back from Tybee, Tyson called Veronica. He complained about his parents taking his SUV, leaving Tyson—sort of stranded.

Tyson picks up Veronica from Motel 6 in his first car that he rode only once this year.

"Let's go play some tennis at the court up the street."

Veronica slumps in the passenger seat. "Boy, you act like you ain't eating."

"Only because mom and dad hit the lottery a few times. We were poor as fuck when we first came here."

"Now, look at you—so blessed."

"Yes, we are." Tyson kisses Veronica's hand and pulls off.

———

Veronica doesn't play tennis often much, but she's competitive. After a few sets, she gives up and starts filming Tyson practice with the tennis ball machine. She uploads videos of him on her Instagram Stories.

"Whatcha doing over there," Tyson said when he sees her recording. "Don't be an Instagram hoe."

"Oh, never that, boo. I'm not Tanya." Veronica chuckles. "Just had to show Mr. Alpha in action."

"The action is when you see my ass moving up and down in the dark."

"I agree but you ain't ready for that."

"I told you, young girl, stop while you're ahead." Tyson signals it's time to go.

———

When Tyson puts the stuff in the car, they walk down to a hole-in-the-wall restaurant named Anne's. Tyson's been there every summer since he was young.

"Anne's got the best fish fry in the A."

"You and your hood eateries." Veronica and Tyson hold hands and Veronica can't help to think how sexy this nigga is.

"It ain't where you from, it's where you at," Tyson said.

"Oh, I see. You're really old-school." Veronica's impressed when she sees the pictures of famous blacks on the restaurant's walls.

They enter and take a table near the door.

———

"I've known this young man since he was yay high," Anne says, pointing to her hip. "All grown up now and bringing these fine girls around. You make me feel like a great-grandmother."

Tyson giggles and Veronica doesn't find it funny.

"Ms., please keep Tyson in line, honey. You ain't the—"

Tyson interrupts, "Ok that's enough, Aunty Anne. We'll have—"

Anne took their orders and left.

"I know exactly what she was going to say, Mr. Tyson," Veronica said looking at her phone.

"I don't know what you're talking about."

"Let's go by my house after we eat. I want to check on my folks."

"I got you."

———

Man-Man and his girl, Stephanie are curled up on the couch watching TV when Tyson and Veronica come over.

It's strange. Veronica's known Stephanie since she was fifteen. They're the same age and went to the same school. Her brother, Man-Man has no swag. She's seen him strike out more times than she can count. That nigga only wants to play video games and smoke weed.

But he's in love and Veronica doesn't know what to say.

Man-Man has his head in Stephanie's lap when they walk in.

"What's up," Man-Man said as Stephanie brushes his waves.

"Hey! What y'all up to?"

"Nothing just watching TV," Stephanie said.

"Where's Mom?"

"You know her. Doing a triple—"

"You mean double, dickhead."

"Watch your mouth, little sis."

"Whatever."

"I see y'all watching reruns of Martin again?" Tyson said making Veronica snicker.

"Hmm...ain't nothing else on, girl," Stephanie said. "What y'all went to Save-a-Lot?"

Man-Man laughed so hard, he almost fell off the couch.

"We played tennis and ate, Ms.—" Veronica said crossing her arms. Tyson stops her just in time before she says something ratchet. "Burgers—"

"Shit, we need some Serena money up in here," Man-Man said. "Go get lost, sis. We're trying to enjoy some Martin."

"I'm going to leave y'all ghetto asses right down where y'all belong. Come on, Tyson."

"Hey, no sex in Mommy's house. You don't live here anymore."

"Fuck you, Man-Man! Yes, I do," Veronica said as she and Tyson go upstairs.

———

Veronica doesn't have a TV in her room.

"Where's your TV?"

"Man-Man and Mama got one. They forgot about me and Shanae."

"You're funny"

"I'm serious." Veronica shoves Tyson when they reach the top of the stairs. "Go take a shower boy, you musky."

———

Veronica slips out of her denim shorts and into a pair of sweats that have seen better days. It's not until she pulls out a shirt from her closet she realizes it's Lamont's. She puts it on anyway.

Tyson gets out of the shower and tries to press up on her. Veronica tells him that her brother will kill her if they fuck while he's still up.

"You're scared of Man-Man?"

"That nigga's crazy." Veronica kisses Tyson before she starts dozing off.

"Sleepy?"

"Yeah, I'm beat." Tyson's hand feels so good rubbing her thigh.

"Stay here if you want."

"Ok."

CHAPTER FOUR

*I*t's the break of dawn when Veronica wakes up and she's sweating bullets. Tyson's still sound asleep curled up behind her. His dick's hard against Veronica's ass, almost near the entrance of her pussy.

Tyson wakes up a few minutes later and she plays like she's still asleep, moving steadily, lest she gives herself away.

"Vee, you awake?"

Veronica hums, "I am now."

"Whose shirt you wearing? Man-Man's? That shit is too big."

"Why you asking me about my shirt this early in the morning I wore your shirt before,"

"So, I can't get an answer?"

"Ok, It was my last boyfriend's and the nigga is long gone, okay?"

"Veronica—" Tyson's hand inches closer to her pussy.

"I'm going to go shower since you don't want

no pussy this morning." She flips the sheets back and walks naked to the bathroom.

"Nah, I was just saying—"

"When you're good, you'll get some." Veronica closes the door behind her.

———

"Ya nigga out back," Man-Man said when Veronica finally comes downstairs in the morning. She tried doing something with her hair and called her mother to make sure she was still at work.

"That ain't my nigga."

"If you don't stop with the bullshit."

Man-Man was making pancakes and Veronica just shakes her head.

"Don't get your mouth watering. They're gluten-free, dairy-free, protein-free pancakes for my boo-boo."

"And that's the first thing a nigga do when he gets some pussy is cook. I got it," Veronica said looking at the stove.

"When are you going to cook for Mr. Tybo?"

"Pussy, you ain't right. Save me some."

———

Veronica makes Tyson a plate and takes it out to him.

"Hey, morning. Is there room for two in your little pity party?"

"You're funny," Tyson said taking the plate. "Where's mom?"

"She'll be home in a few hours. She's doing doubles again."

"Then we got some time," Tyson said with a mouthful of pancake.

"Nah, I'm going to the YMCA."

"Where?"

"Up the street."

————

They drive in Veronica's sister Shanae's Lexus to the Y.

"You still mad, huh?" Veronica said bumping her head to the radio.

"I'm good."

"No, you're not. When you be good, mommy will give you some."

"That's a new rule?"

"You'll get it." Veronica leans over and kisses Tyson on the cheek

————

Veronica and Tyson go for a swim before they work out. After their workout, they get in the jacuzzi.

"How often do you come here?" Tyson said kicking off his sandals before getting in.

"Not often. My mother used to take us here at least once a month when we first came from Miami."

"It's a good place for young people," Tyson said.

"Yeah, Man-Man, Shanae and I would beat each other in the car on the way down here."

"Y'all crazy!"

"Y'all crazy."

CHAPTER FIVE

Veronica starts her first semester at Georgia Tech and can't wait until she goes on winter break. The few holidays she had, she'd spent working part-time. Her sister Letisha, Cousins Shanae and Lamar and Lisa often come up to visit her until Christmas break.

On Christmas Eve, Veronica's Mom cooked and baked with Shanae and Lisa while Tyson and Veronica went out with Lamar and Stephanie. They came home drunk and almost slept on Christmas morning until their aunt, Marsha rang the doorbell. She brought some presents and bottles of liquor.

"Hurry up girl," Mom said as Veronica slowly unwrapped her present; a pair of silk pajamas. "I hope you like them," Aunt Marsha said.

"She'll wear them tonight," Tyson said knowing how bad they looked.

"I'll keep them for a special occasion." Veronica stuck her tongue out at Tyson.

———

The family had a late breakfast and then Tyson and Lamar took over the TV to play Madden on PS4. Veronica's cousin Lamar kept starting over the game because he kept losing. Tyson put him in a headlock and Mom yelled from upstairs for them to knock it off.

Veronica comes in the room and Tyson threw his controller at Lamar.

"Is Letisha excited about going to Spelman?" Tyson asks.

"I think so." Veronica plays with her hair. "You know I think about where we're going with this all time."

"You act like you're fifty years old."

"Tyson, I'm serious. Why didn't we talk while you were staying on campus? What if I fucked somebody else?"

"Veronica, it's Christmas—"

"I know but—"

"I don't know. I can't remember…"

"So, you dumped Tanya for me?"

"I did."

"So what are you going to do with me?" Veronica grabs Tyson's crotch.

"Whatever you want."

———

"We'll be back. Veronica yells from the patio.

"Don't be out too long. Dinner is almost ready."

"Ok, Mom."

Veronica tells Tyson they're going to the park.

"Are you kidnapping me?"

"I am because I want to share a secret with you."

"Hmm. Ok.

"Good. Will you be good?

"Yes."

"You'll find out later if you are."

Tyson stares at Veronica's ass while she dusts the dirt off her shorts. "Girl, you got a booty."

"I know. Ready to head back?" Veronica starts jogging.

"Wrong way…"

"I know where I'm going. Just run."

Tyson catches up and smacks her on the booty.

"Boy, stop! People looking."

"See you're not being good."

"I'm sorry."

———

It starts raining as soon when they reach Veronica's house. She drops her keys and Tyson took them.

"Boy, give me my keys. You play too much."

"Race you from here to the corner. If you win, I'll give them back."

"Boy, I'll dust you!"

———

Veronica beat Tyson and they go inside soaking wet. After Veronica dries off, she helps Lisa with making the potato salad. Lamar and Tyson are on the patio, grilling the last of the steaks.

"Did you have fun today?" Lisa asks.

"Yeah, we did."

"Things are moving along with Mr. Tyboo, I see."

"Girl, we cool. Ain't nothing serious yet."

"Just friends, huh?"

"Yeah!"

"Well, y'all been hanging out since before you left."

"I know, girl. You're so nosey."

"You don't have to mention the details.

Veronica laughs. "Nah, it ain't like that. He's with me sometimes and ain't. It's hard to explain."

"I hear you. Guess what?"

"What?"

"I heard Tyson's old girl Tanya's strippin' now

cos she couldn't get enough money to go to college."

"Damn, that's fucked up."

"Yeah, I thought you knew."

"Nah."

"Well, ain't nothing to worry about now. Better keep that nigga cos he's fine as fuck."

"I guess."

"I don't wanna see you hurt, boo." Lisa hugs her and they finish making the salad.

———

Later that evening, Veronica did something she never did before. She let Tyson in her room while her mom was home.

Tyson was too drunk to drive back and slept after dinner.

"Tyson's still up there knocked out?" Veronica's mother said.

"Yeah! What y'all been doing?"

"Nothing, ma!"

"Don't let me hear y'all having sex in my house."

"Ma, ain't nobody doing anything! Excuse y'all, let me go check on Tyson."

"You see your daughter," Aunt Brenda said.

"Sis, she acts just like you."

CHAPTER SIX

*I*t's just after two in the morning and everyone is in bed. Veronica wakes up telling Tyson he has to go home before her mom wakes up in the morning. She drives him to his parents' home and Tyson convinces her to sleep there. Tyson's parents are asleep and he told her to go to his sister's room.

Veronica tried sleeping but she can't. She went down the hall to Tyson's room finding it unlocked. Tyson's snoring. She goes inside, closed the door and leans against it to make sure it's locked.

"Tyson?" Veronica takes off her clothes. "Tyson?" Then she slips under the covers beside him.

He's sleeping good and hums. "Vee, what you doing in here?"

Veronica caresses his balls.

"Vee—Oh my God!"

"Shut the fuck up. You talk too much. Lay back and relax."

Veronica massages his balls and Tyson moans.

"What do you want mommy to do, boo?"

"I want to—Oh! Oh! Right there! Shit..."

Veronica goes under the sheets and starts sucking his dick. The slobber from her mouth dampens under Tyson's spot. He squirms as she bobs up and down.

"I'm about to—"

Veronica stops.

"Why you stop?

"I want you to give me what I want and stop playing these games with me. I told you boy that mommy will treat you good if you're good."

"I'm being good—"

"I'm not convinced yet." Veronica starts sucking again and tastes Tyson's about to cum. She stops again.

"What the fuck, Vee!"

"I thought you wanted me, Mr. Tyson. Why you playing these games with me?"

"I'm not."

"You ain't givin' me all of you. You think I'm young and dumb. I haven't forgotten about your stripper bitch Tanya."

"I'm done with that."

"Did she strip for you?"

"You're funny. No, I don't know what you talkin' about."

"Yeah, right. You're still holdin' back." Veronica goes back down and gags on his balls while jerking his dick. Tyson's about to cum again and Veronica stops.

"You're killing me. What the fuck!"

"I know because you're not being a good boy."

"I am—"

"I'm not convinced yet."

Veronica goes back down and this time she sucks slower. His pre-ejaculation reminds her of Arm & Hammer toothpaste. If she moves a sec faster, he'll cum all down her throat. She wants that and finally gives him what he wants. Tyson cums and Veronica licks it all and swallows. Tyson's dick is still hard.

"Why ya dick is still hard?"

"I don't know. You tell me." Tyson took some Viagra earlier that the day thinking he was going to get some.

"I asked you why ya dick still hard?"

"I said I don't know."

Veronica puts her pussy on top of Tyson's face. "Eat my pussy, Daddy."

Her pussy is so wet that she starts shaking as soon as his tongue touches her clit.

"Damn, mommy! You cummin' already. I didn't even hit yet!"

"I told you boy if you're good, I'm good. Eat some more of my pussy."

Tyson licks again, sucking on her walls.

"God, yeah. Eat it, daddy! Oh my God! You are so—I'm cumming again..."

The noises coming out of her mouth are hard to make out. Tyson grabs on her nipple and Veronica feels helpless.

"Oh shit! Oh shit! Not again...?" Veronica came again.

"Get up!"

"What?"

"You heard what I said."

"Ok, Daddy."

Tyson spreads Veronica's legs and puts his dick inside her without a rubber.

"You're still on the pill, right?"

"Yeah, boy. Now you ask me."

Veronica says Tyson's name for the fiftieth time as Tyson kept stroking all night long until the roosters crow.

CHAPTER SEVEN

Veronica back on campus after the Christmas break. It's a new semester and Tyson comes by to bring her some supplies.

"Where've you been? Damn, you take all day," Veronica said, looking up from her math homework.

"Hanging out with a couple of people from your school. We went to play pool in the rec room."

"I heard."

"How?"

"Snapchat, nigga! By the way, Shantay's in my English class."

"Ok, so—"

"Didn't think she was into you," Veronica said, clearing a formula from her calculator.

"I didn't think she so, either. But—"

"She posted that you treated her to some ice cream after the game."

"I treated everybody."

"And DM'ed Letisha, saying y'all went back to her dorm room and you ate her pussy."

"That's a lying hoe."

"I don't know about that. So, tell me what really happened."

Veronica put her pencil down and turned.

"Ok, you may peak."

"So—Shantay said she needed a ride home. I'm like okay and on the way, she said she had to use the bathroom. I told her we'll stop at Grindhouse but she said didn't want to use their dirty-ass bathrooms. I told her I'll take her over my spot to go. I waited for her to come out and when she did, she was naked. I told her I was cool but she grabbed me by the dick—"

"And?"

"And she sucked it, I fucked her and I didn't eat her pussy."

"That's it, right?"

"Sike!"

Veronica punched Tyson in the arm. "Nigga, you are so wrong."

"I knew you were lying. I told you Coach had us stay late for practice."

———

Tyson comes from behind Veronica and tells her to spread her legs. Her roommate isn't there for the weekend. He kisses her on the neck and then puts his fingers inside her pussy, fingering her lightly. Her walls clench down on them and she moans as Tyson goes in and out.

When she cums, her fingernails dig into Tyson's neck.

"Now, who's going to be good? Tyson kisses Veronica on the neck and still keeps fingering.

"Oh, yes. I will, Daddy—Damn, I will —Please—"

"I know." Tyson stops fingering her and Veronica grabs his hand and licks his fingers.

"It's all you, Mommy."

"Don't be playin' me, okay?"

"I won't."

"Love you, Tyson."

"That got you loving me baby, huh?"

"Yes."

Tyson's dick is now piercing his jeans.

"Come here. I want some of that."

Tyson unbuttons his jeans and Veronica sucks, her slobber falls on the floor and on Tyson's Timbs.

"You like this, daddy?" Tyson shivers.

"Hell, yeah!"

Veronica licks it like a popsicle, not believing how long Tyson's dick is.

"My brother, always this long, huh?" Veronica said as she wraps both hands around his dick.

"For you." Tyson feels he's about to nut.

"What, boo? Mommy got you about to cum.."

"Yeah, yeah! Oh shit! Stop!"

Veronica stops.

"What is it?"

"I want that dick inside of me."

"Again with no rubber..."

Veronica puts her hand on her head.

"You ain't got HIV. Do you?"

"No."

"Okay, then stop asking questions."

"And that's it."

"I'm on the pill, anyway, fool."

Veronica pulls down her skirt and Tyson sits in her chair riding him up and down.

"Oh my God! That pussy is—."

Veronica clenches him as the pleasure zips up her spine.

"You're ready to cum in me, Daddy?

"Please, stop! Oh my God!"

Veronica works her magic into a slow, steady rhythm, kissing Tyson and putting her tongue in his ear. It feels so good and he's saying 'I love you' and the rest of the words of love in the English language.

Tyson tries to pull out when he feels he's about to nut.

"Keep fucking me, Daddy. Don't worry about that. I got you." Veronica's nails are planted on his shoulder tips. Tyson thrusts become faster and Veronica's moaning his name, "Tyson, Tyson, Tyson..." She's cumming and he's almost there.

"Oh, Vee, Oh, Vee—" Tyson moans trying to pull out again as he strokes.

"Daddy, cum in me. It's all yours."

Tyson grabs her ass and thrusts; his eyes are closed and he's sweating. Veronica feels the warmness of his cum coming out and Tyson's shaking left and right.

"Oh! Oh! Oh!"

Veronica rubs her pussy, kisses him and cums again with him. Then, she got up to warm a rag.

"I can't believe you came inside me, boy."

"Why's that? You said you were on the pill."

"Do you believe all the girls when they say that?"

"Vee, don't fuck with me. You on the pill or not?"

"I am."

She grabs his hand and puts it on her pussy.

"You feel that, Daddy?"

"I do."

———

They chill out for the rest of the evening, watching Netflix and eating pizza. Meanwhile, the suspense lingers on in Tyson's mind whether or not Veronica's really on the pill.

CHAPTER EIGHT

*I*t's 8:30 AM on Sunday morning. Veronica wakes up and shakes Tyson.

"Hey, what are you still doing here?"

"I fell asleep."

"Sure, creep."

"Well, you know it's time to go. My roommate came back."

"I'm not going yet," Tyson kisses Veronica.

"I think you might want to—"

Tyson hears pans clinging in the kitchen.

"Who's in the kitchen?"

"My woman."

"Say what? Get the fuck outta here. You're joking."

"I'm not," Veronica calls her roommate to her bedroom.

"Stop fucking playing."

"I'm not."

The girl comes inside with her bra and panties on. It's the teammate, Veronica was sneaking around with in high school, who ate her pussy.

"Hi, Tyson. I heard a lot about you."

"Hi—" Tyson looks at Veronica and she winks.

"Why you looking at my girl like that?" Veronica said.

"I'm not—"

"Come in, Leah."

Leah comes in and closes the door.

"Leah, let me introduce you to Tyson," Veronica said pulling off the sheets. Tyson's dick is hard as a rock poking up.

Leah climbs in bed and kisses Veronica.

"Round three?" Tyson said.

"If you can keep your mouth closed."

"Yes, ma'am."

Leah and Veronica go down on Tyson and he grabs the headrest behind. As they lick and suck his dick, he wonders whether Veronica was fucking with him about being on the pill or not. For sure, his young thing will get knocked up soon and maybe her roommate, too.

9 781925 988178